NIGHTMARE SCHMIGHTMARE

WRITTEN AND ILLUSTRATED BY
SPENCER PLATT

ISBN: 978-0692389522

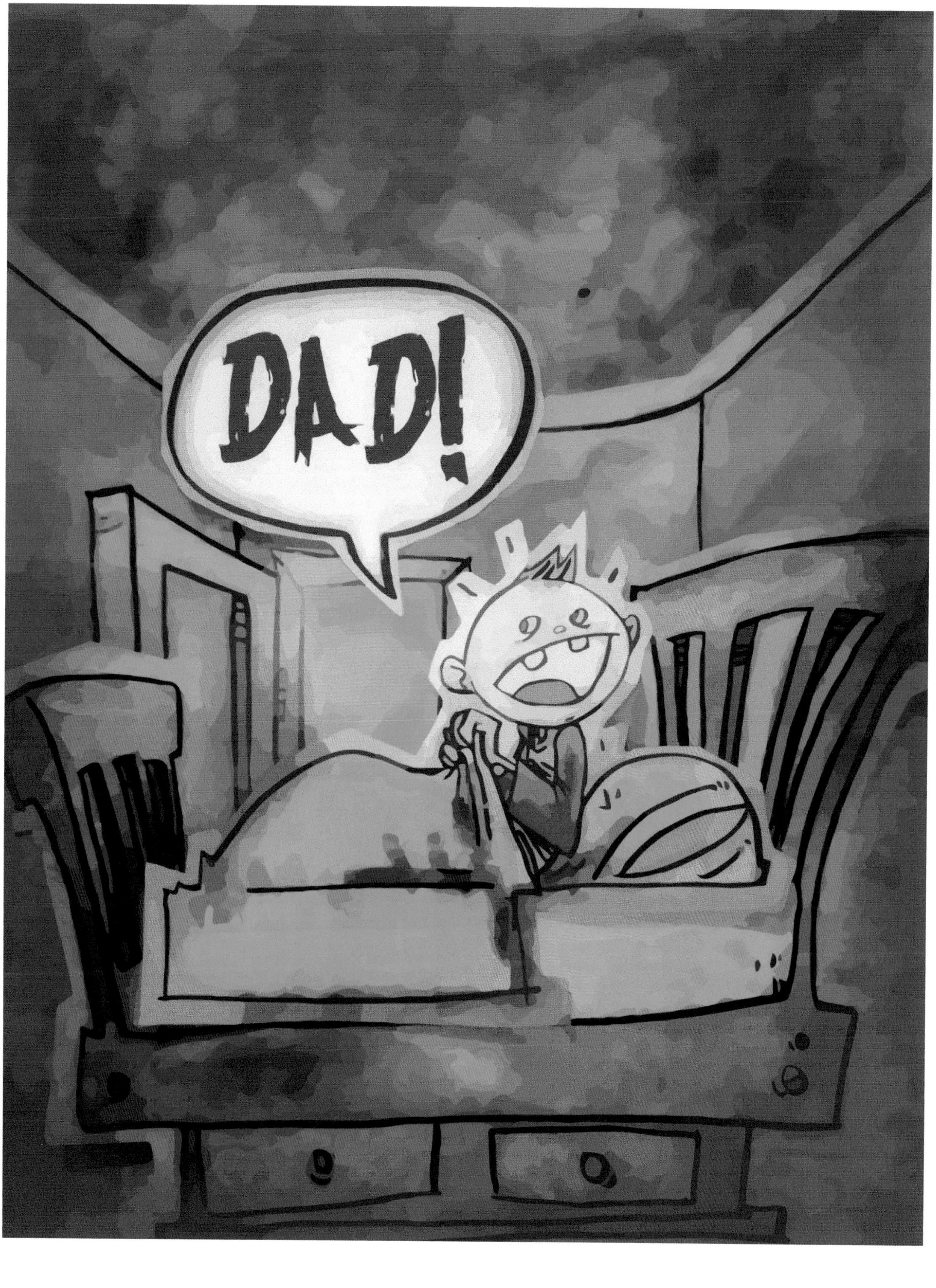
DAD!

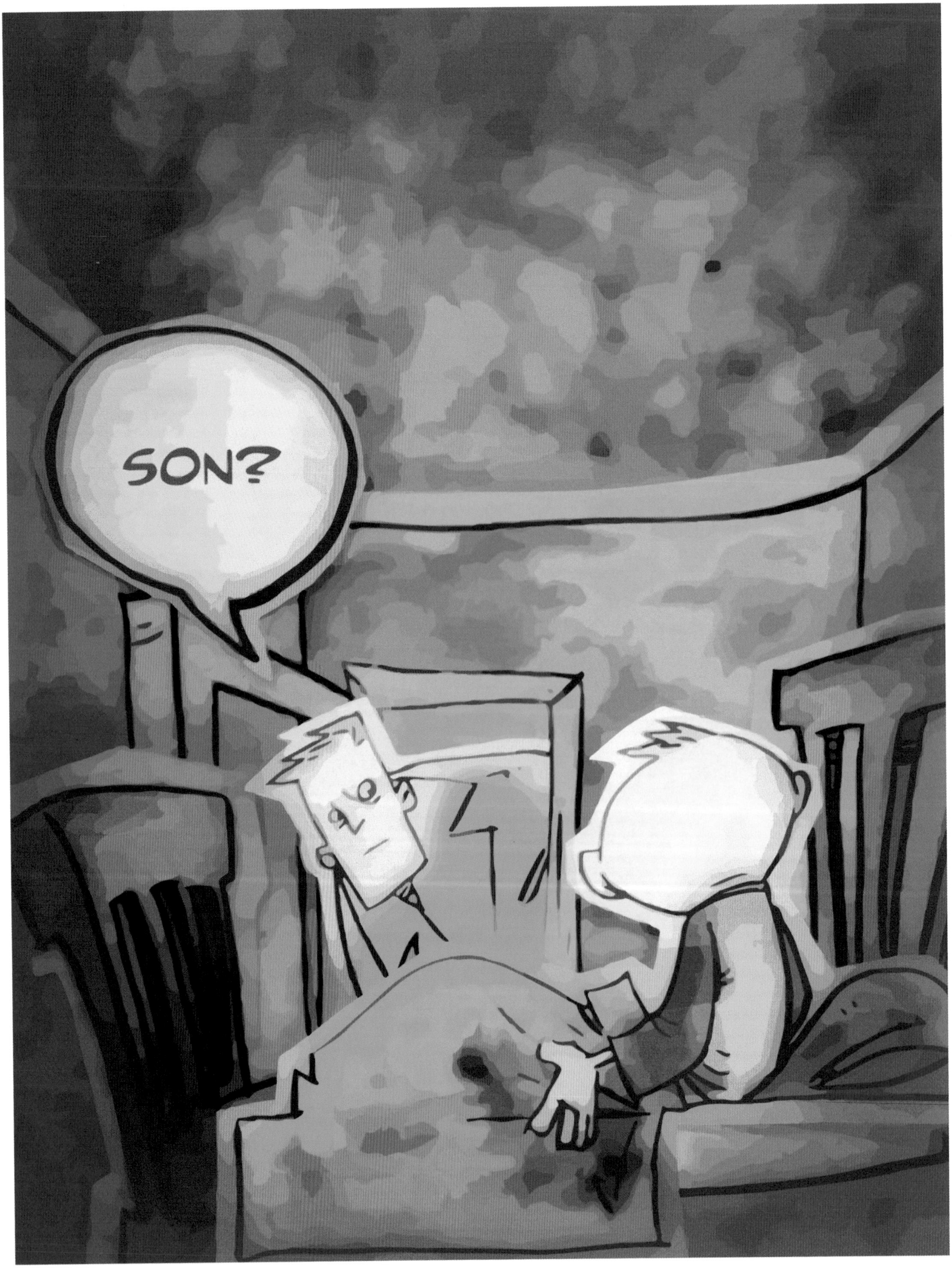
SON?

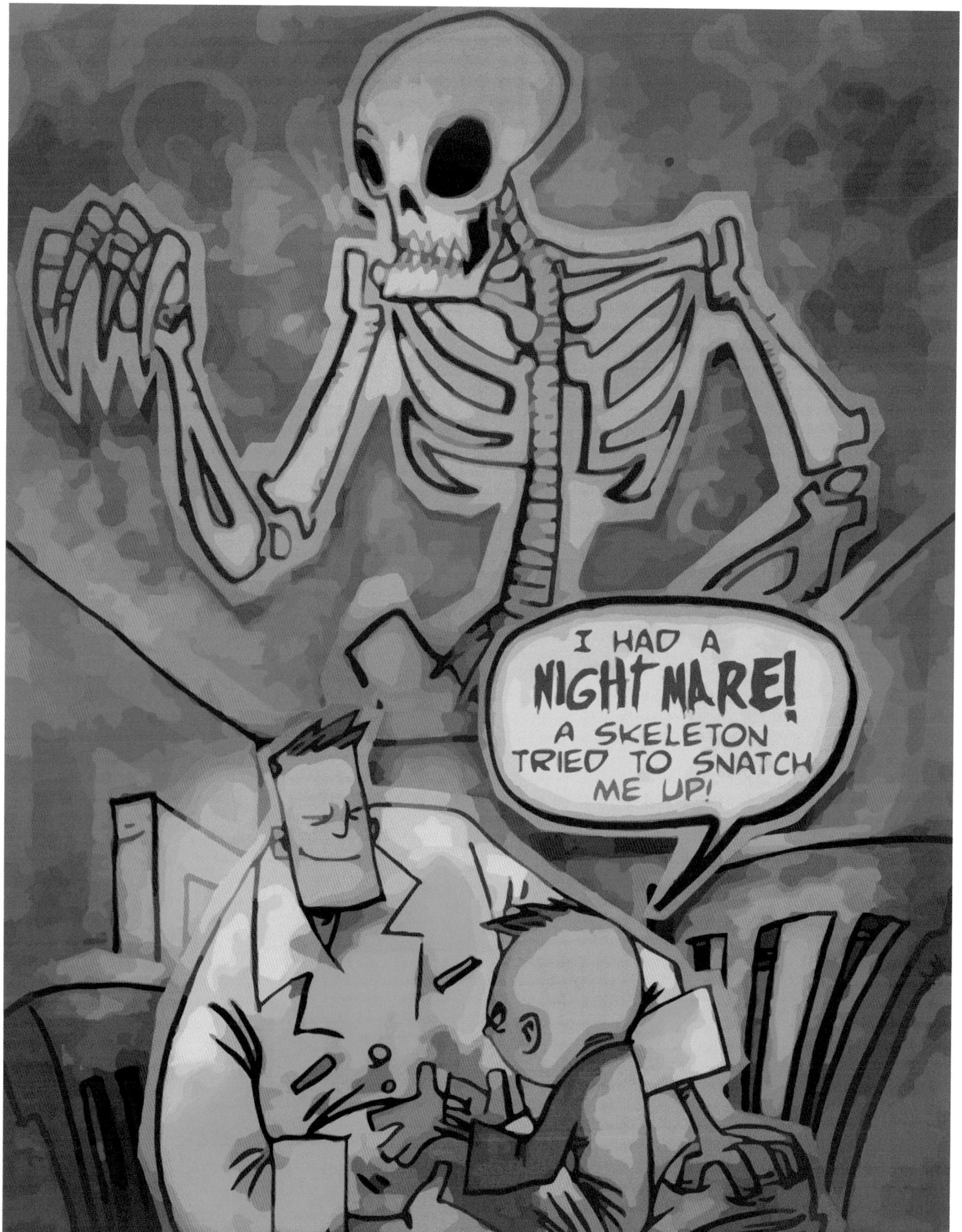
I HAD A NIGHTMARE! A SKELETON TRIED TO SNATCH ME UP!

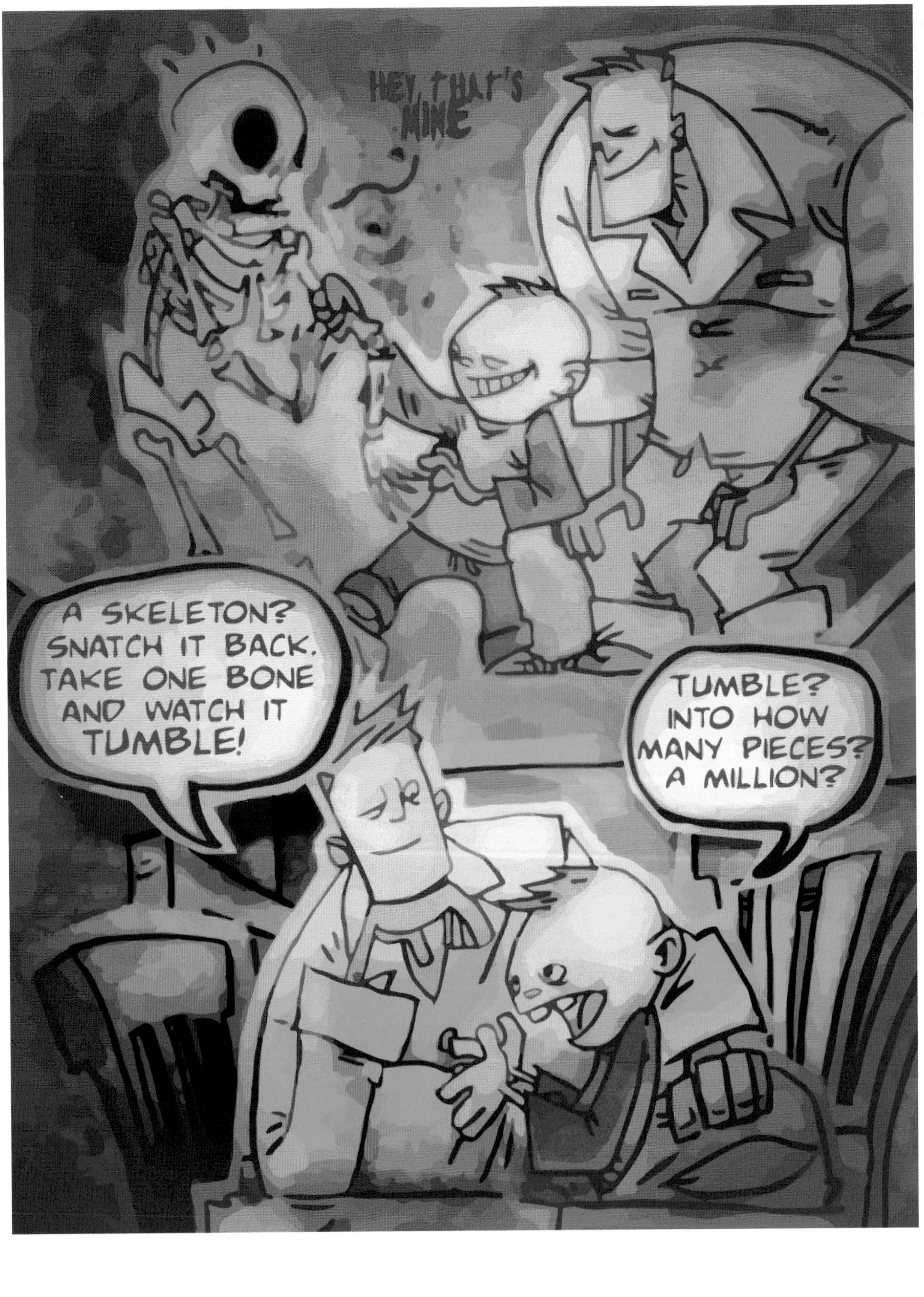
HEY THAT'S MINE
A SKELETON? SNATCH IT BACK. TAKE ONE BONE AND WATCH IT TUMBLE!
TUMBLE? INTO HOW MANY PIECES? A MILLION?

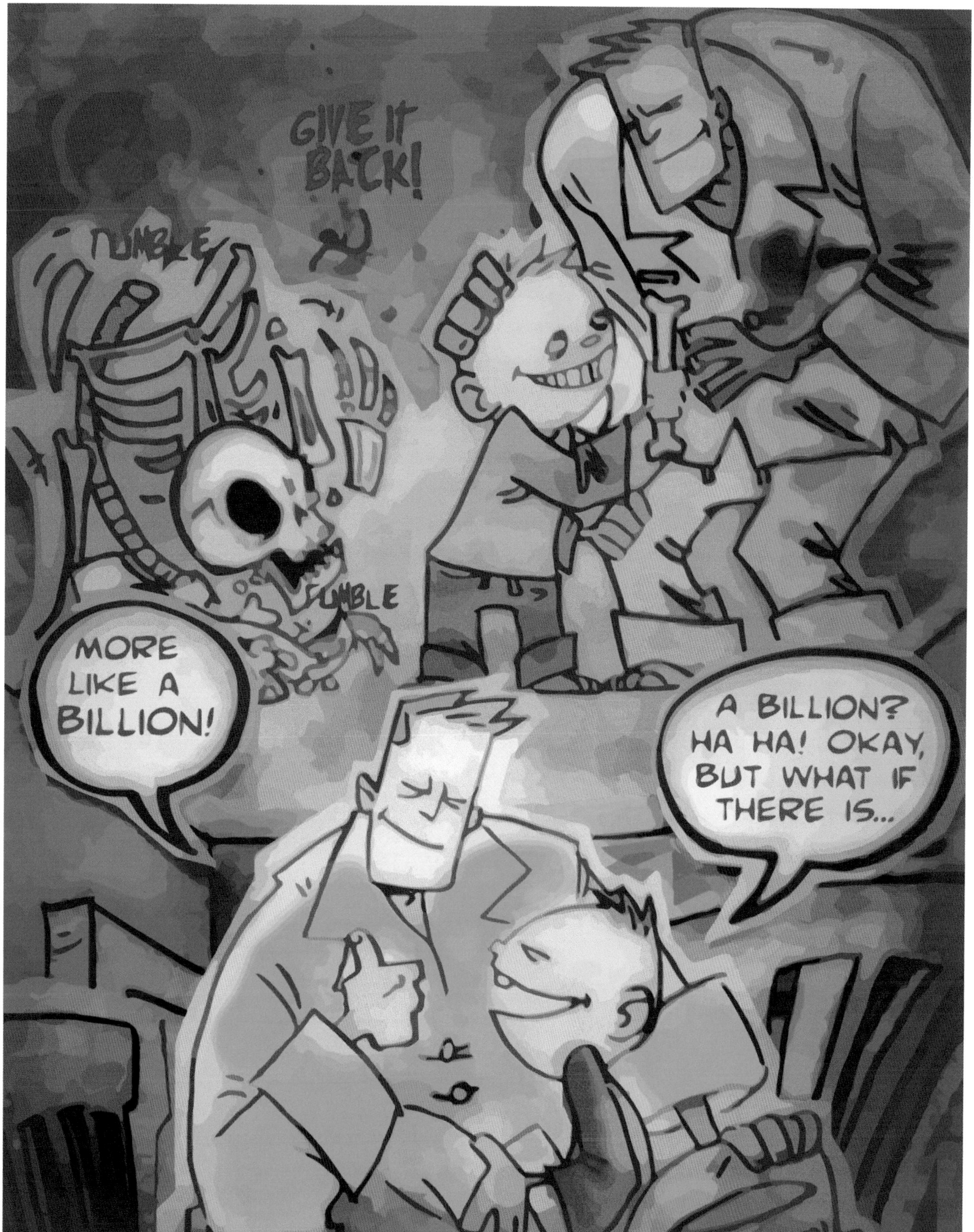
GIVE IT BACK!
TUMBLE
TUMBLE
MORE LIKE A BILLION!
A BILLION? HA HA! OKAY, BUT WHAT IF THERE IS...

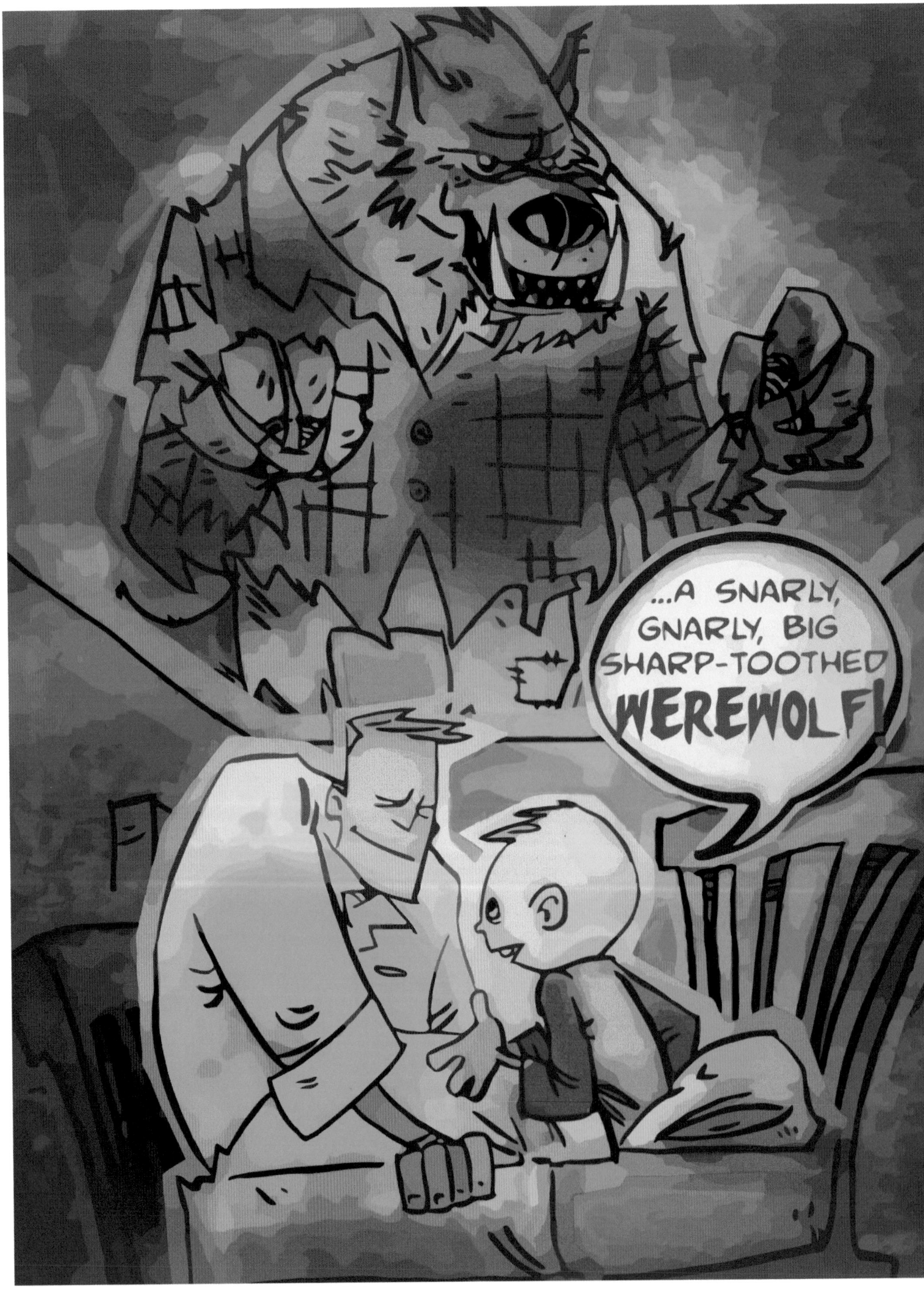
...A SNARLY, GNARLY, BIG SHARP-TOOTHED WEREWOLF!

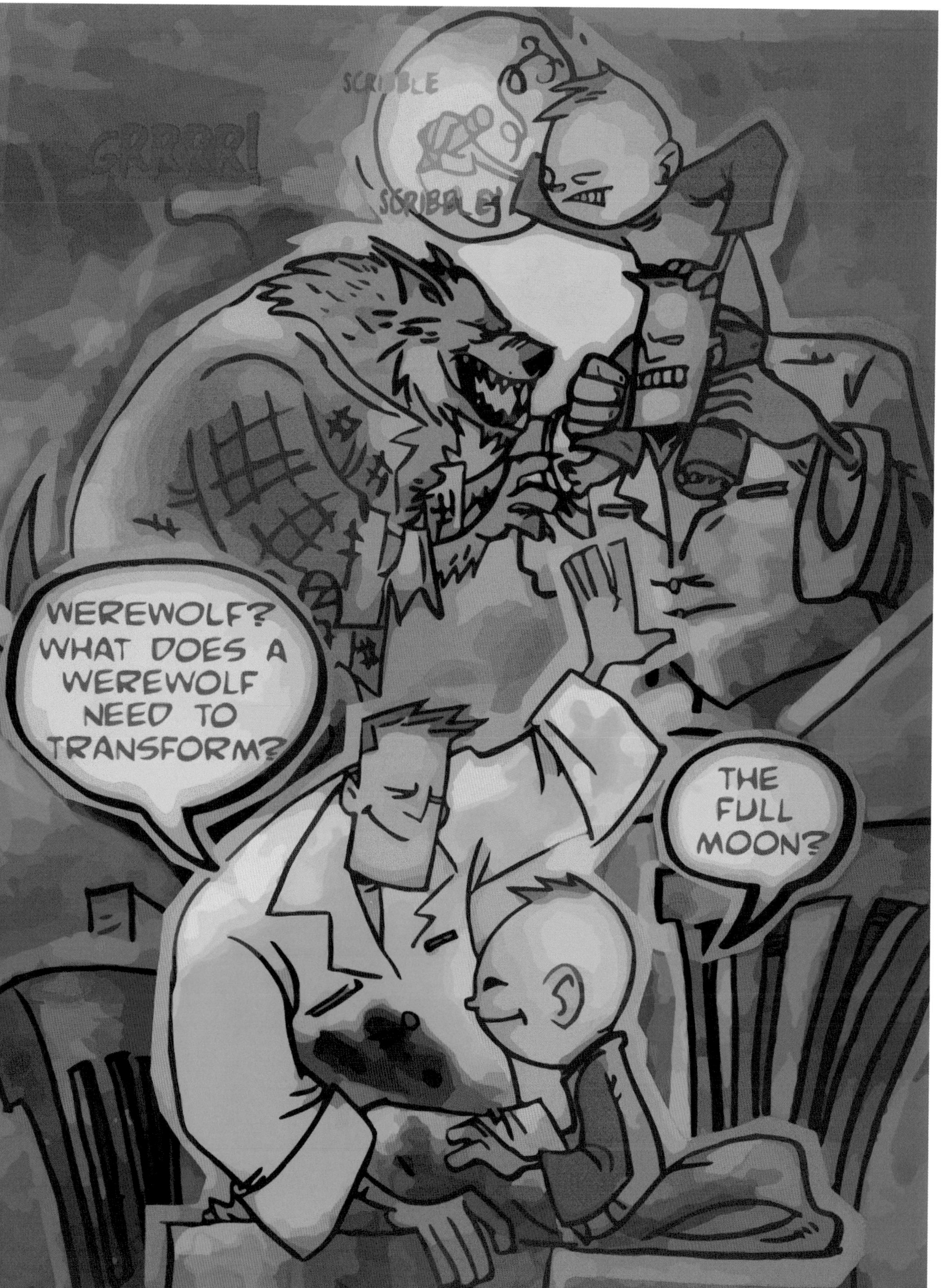
SCRIBBLE
GRRRR!
SCRIBBLE!
WEREWOLF? WHAT DOES A WEREWOLF NEED TO TRANSFORM?
THE FULL MOON?

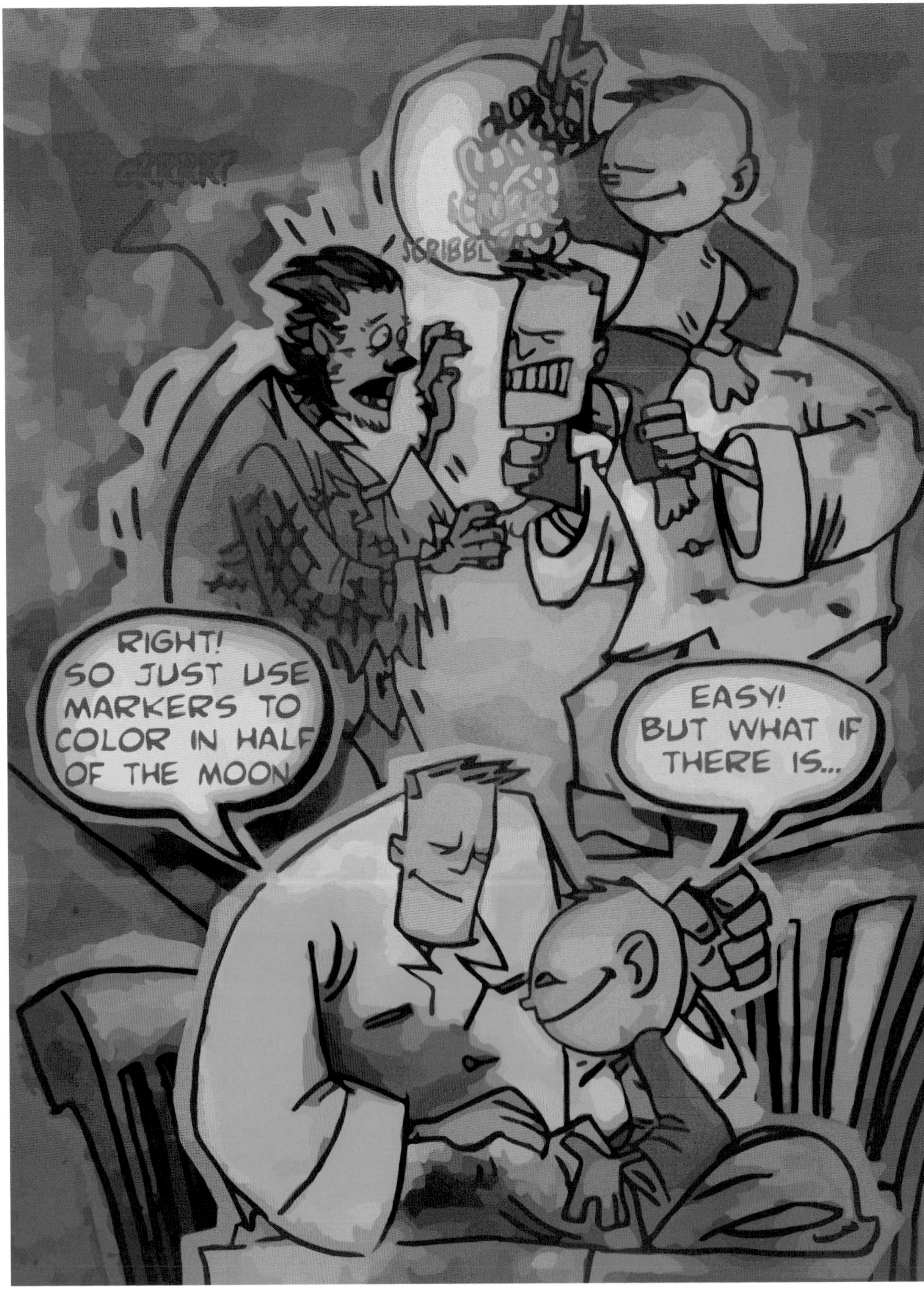
RIGHT! SO JUST USE MARKERS TO COLOR IN HALF OF THE MOON
EASY! BUT WHAT IF THERE IS...

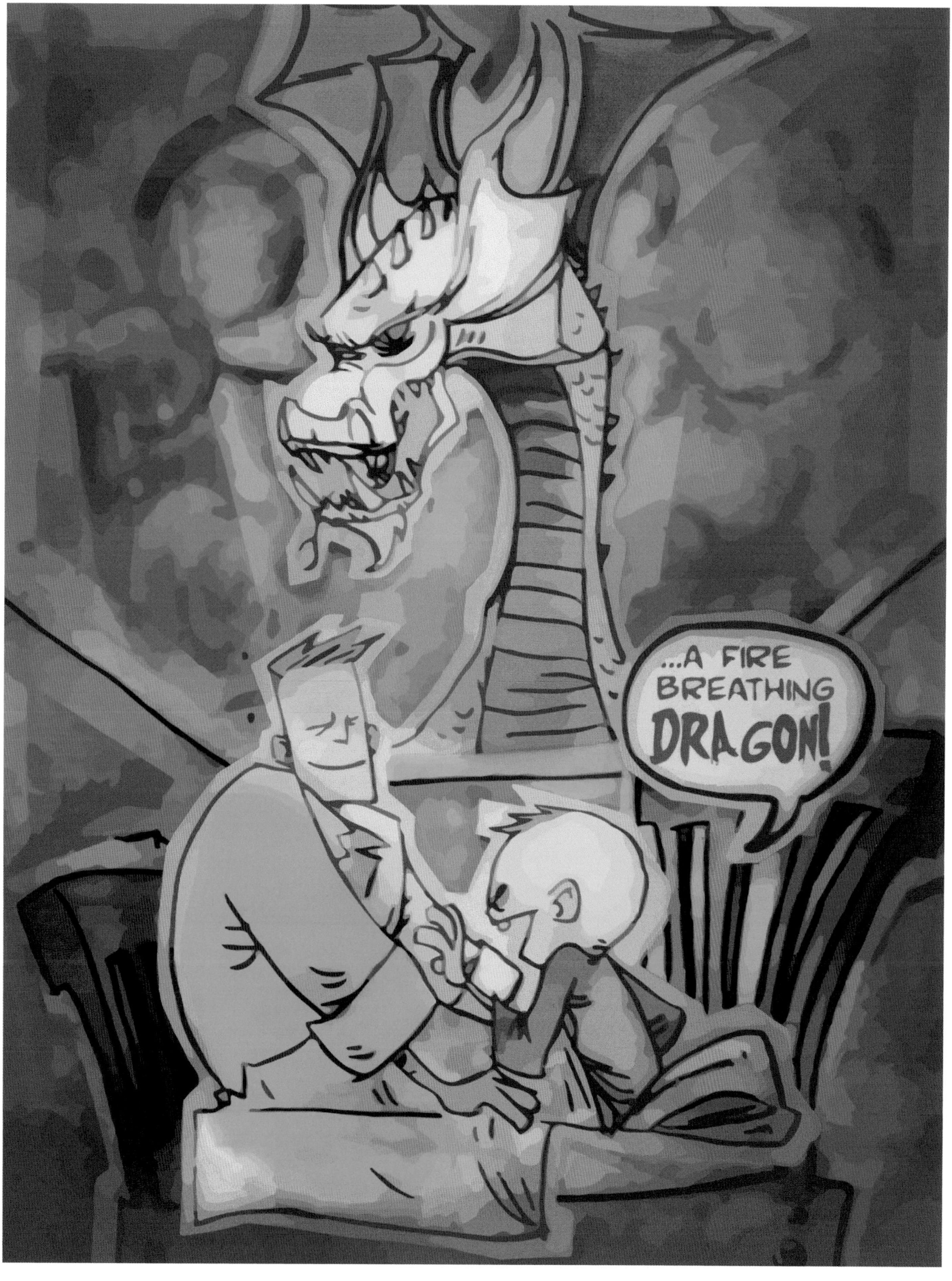
...A FIRE BREATHING DRAGON!

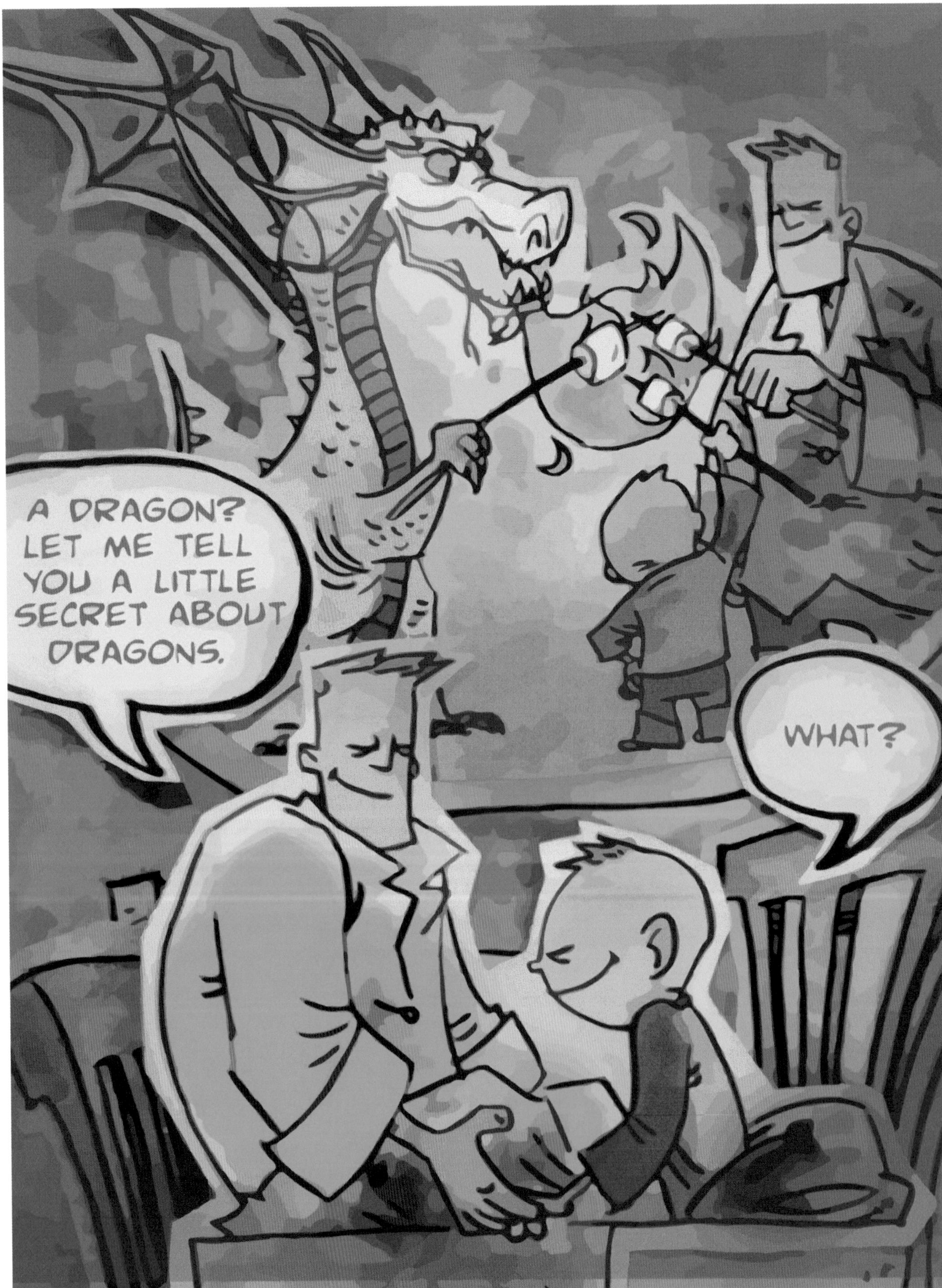
A DRAGON? LET ME TELL YOU A LITTLE SECRET ABOUT DRAGONS.
WHAT?

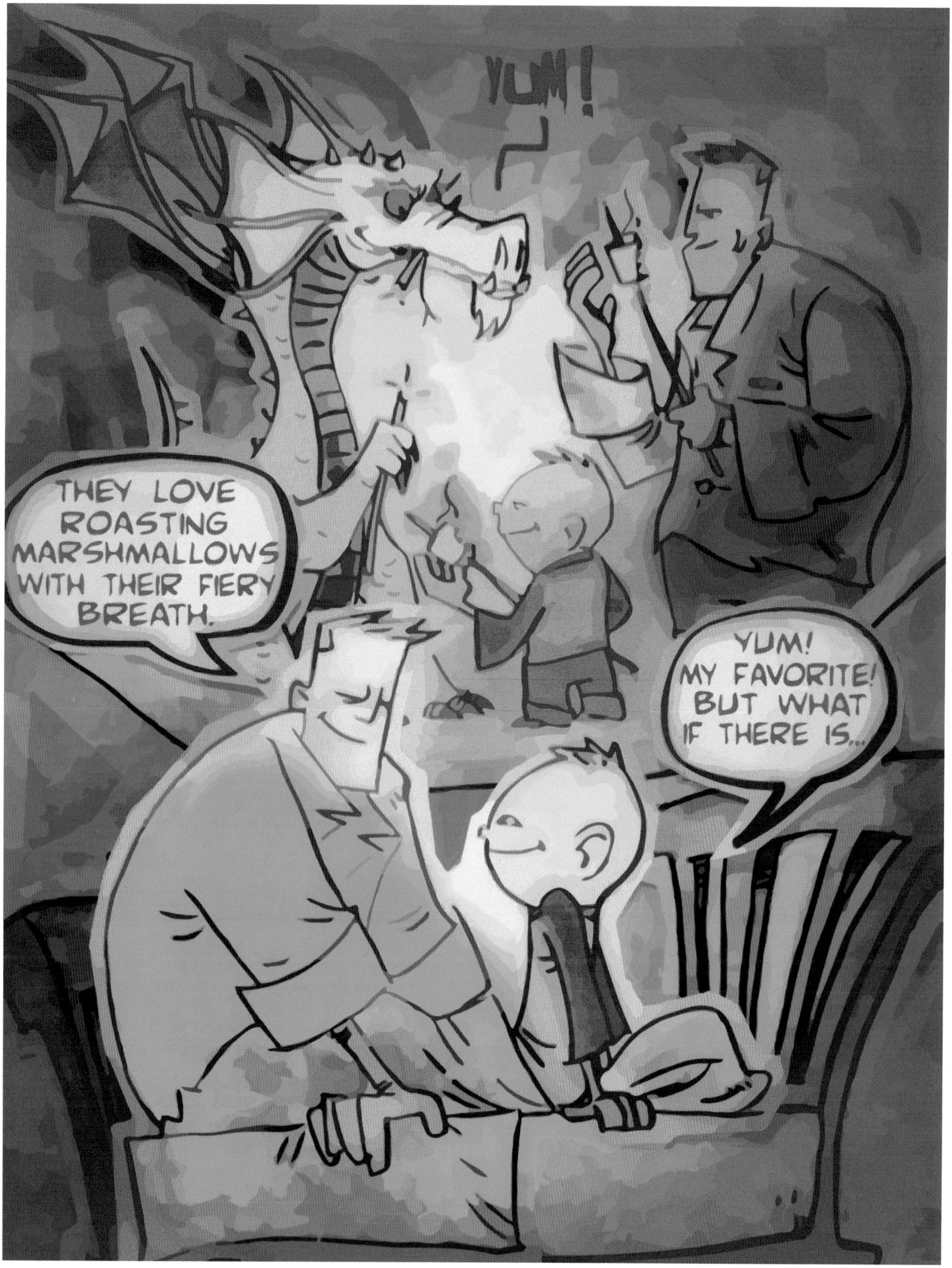
YUM!
THEY LOVE ROASTING MARSHMALLOWS WITH THEIR FIERY BREATH.
YUM! MY FAVORITE! BUT WHAT IF THERE IS...

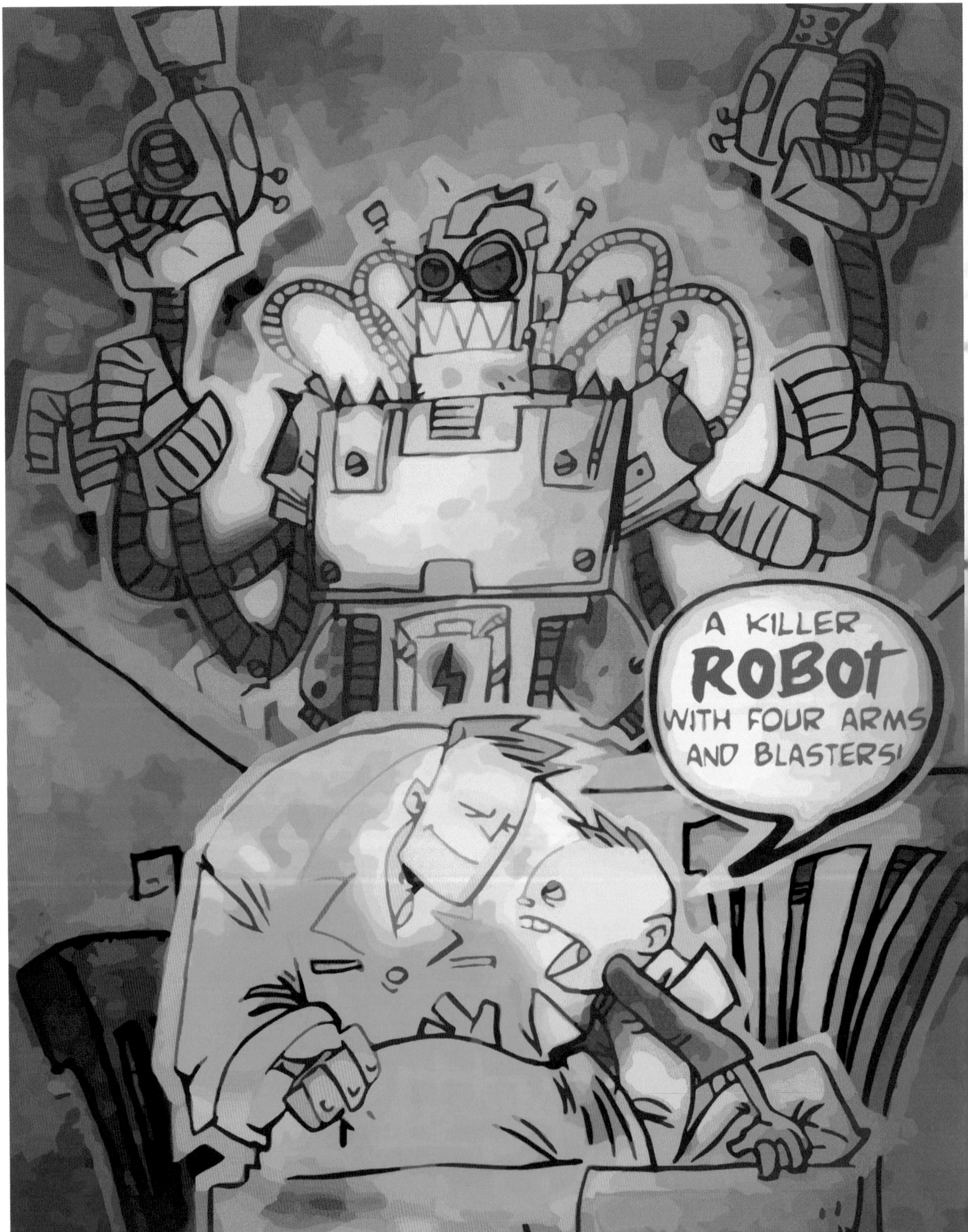
A KILLER ROBOT WITH FOUR ARMS AND BLASTERS!

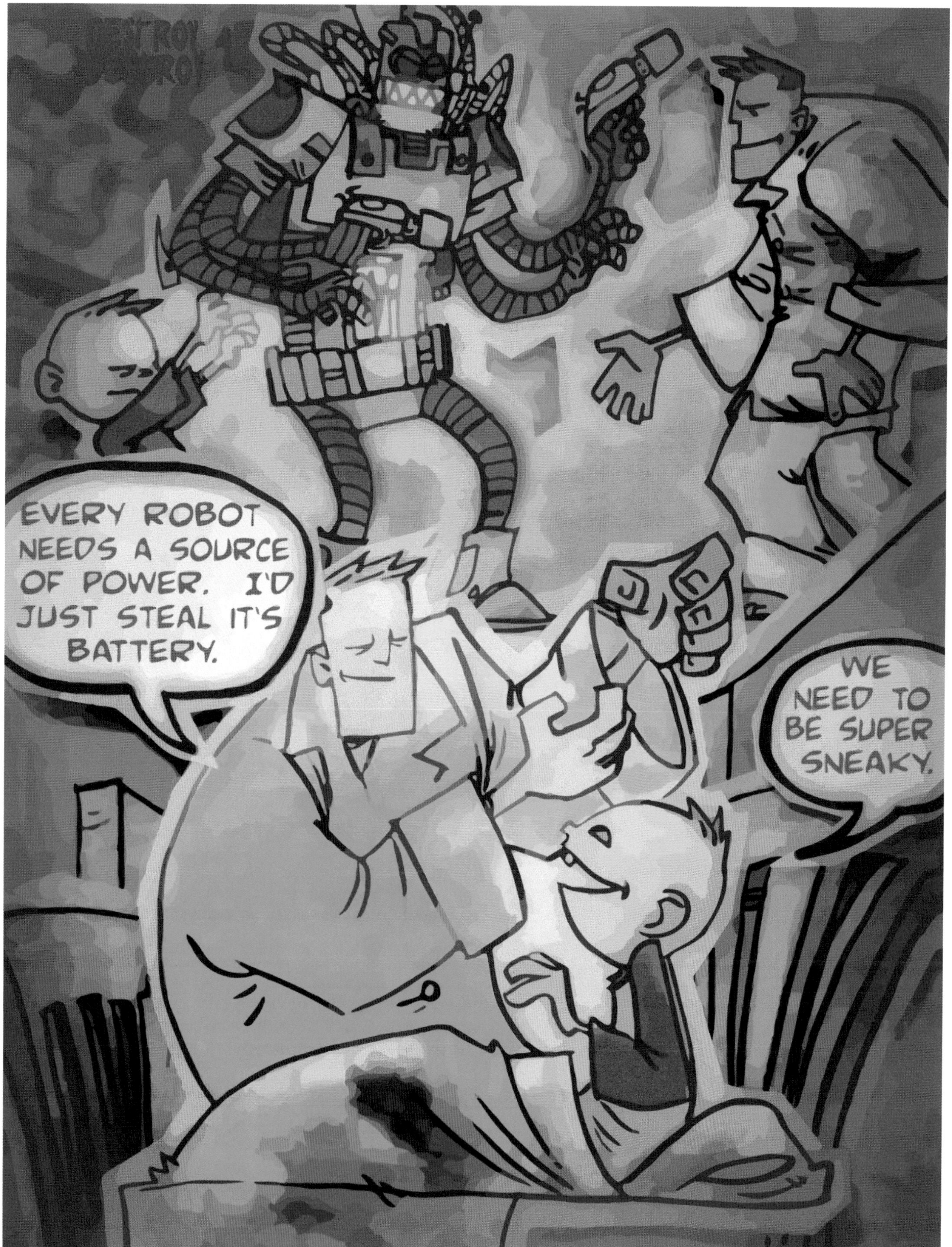
EVERY ROBOT NEEDS A SOURCE OF POWER. I'D JUST STEAL IT'S BATTERY.
WE NEED TO BE SUPER SNEAKY.

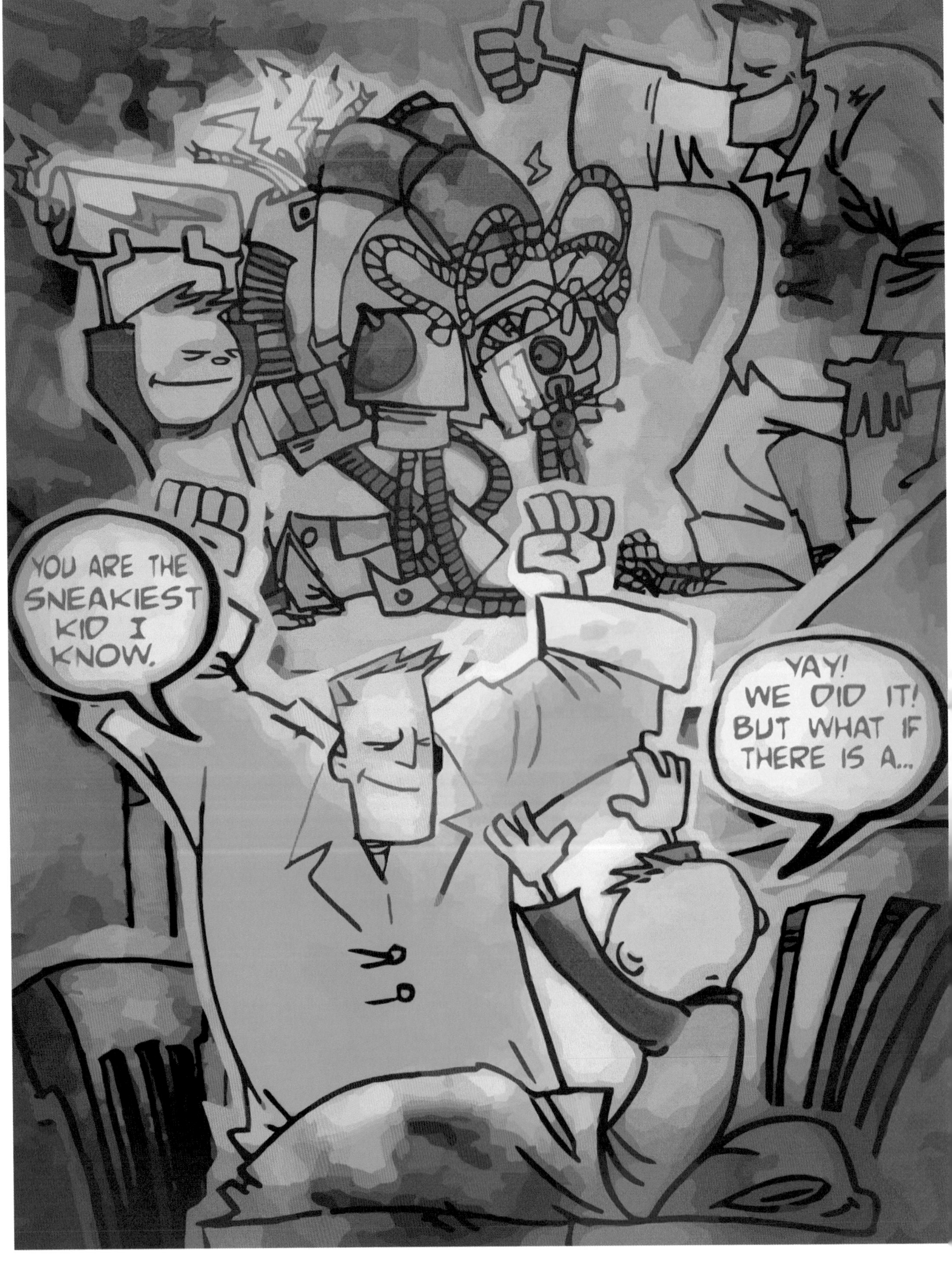
YOU ARE THE SNEAKIEST KID I KNOW.
YAY! WE DID IT! BUT WHAT IF THERE IS A...

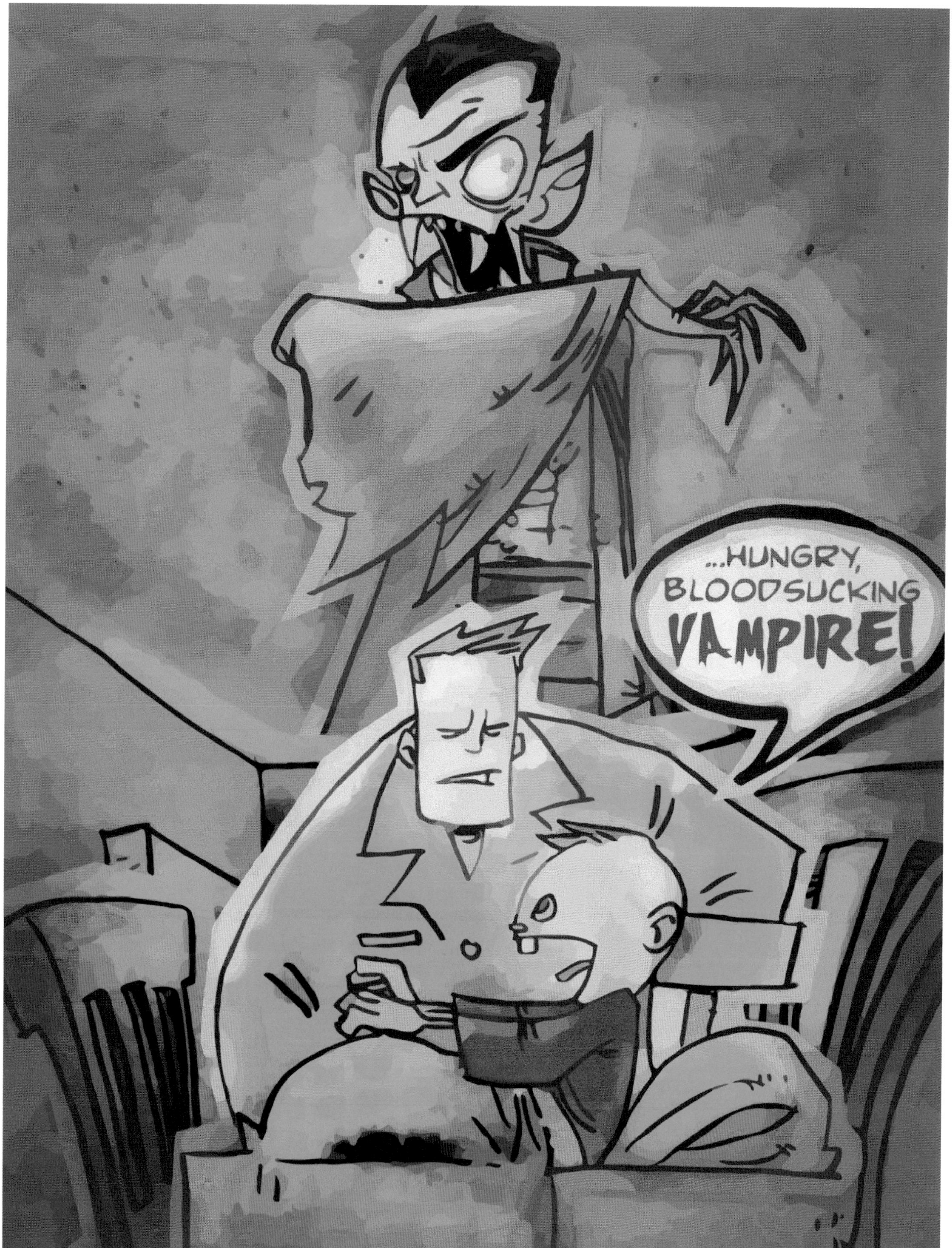
...HUNGRY, BLOODSUCKING VAMPIRE!

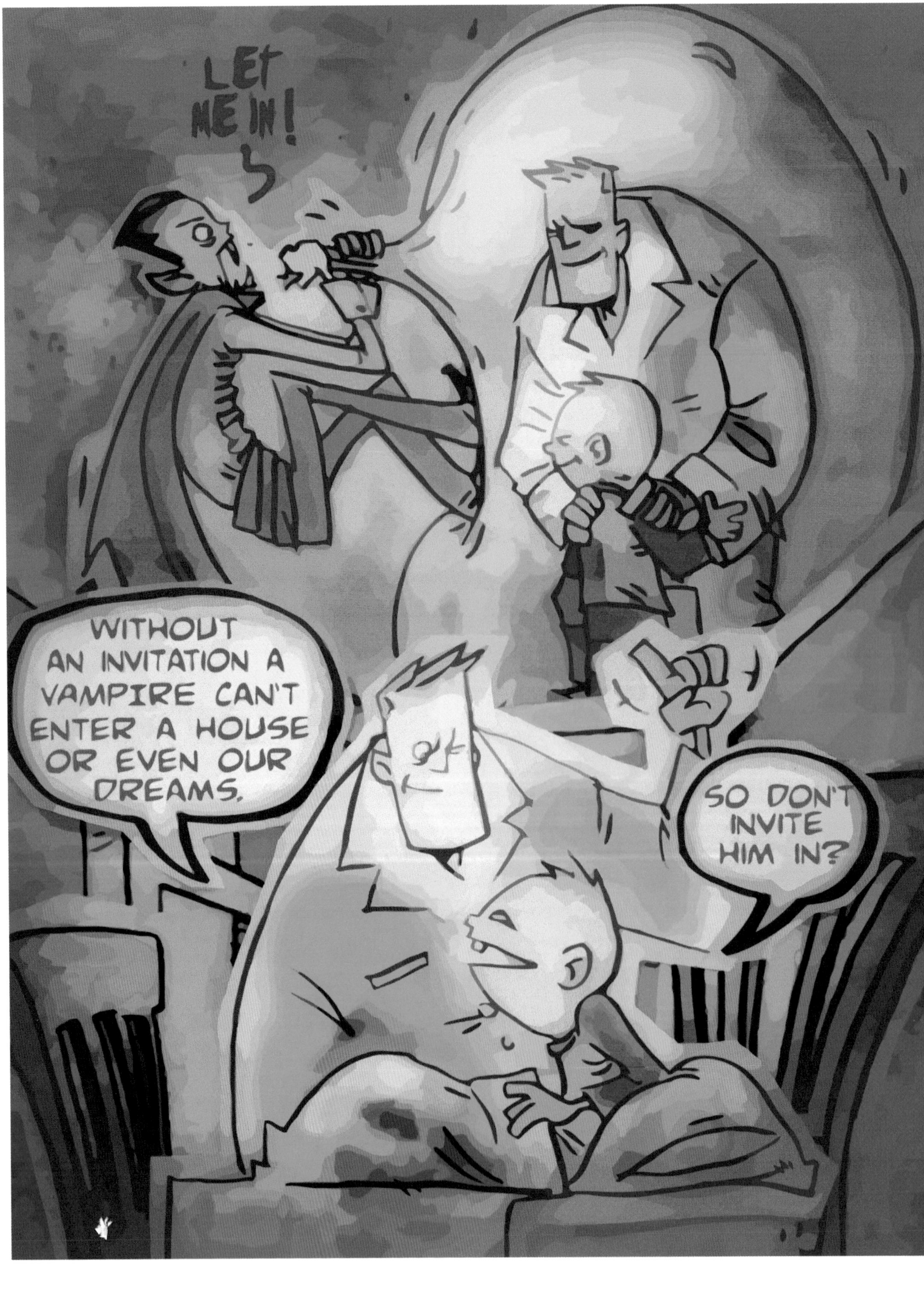
LET ME IN!
WITHOUT AN INVITATION A VAMPIRE CAN'T ENTER A HOUSE OR EVEN OUR DREAMS.
SO DON'T INVITE HIM IN?

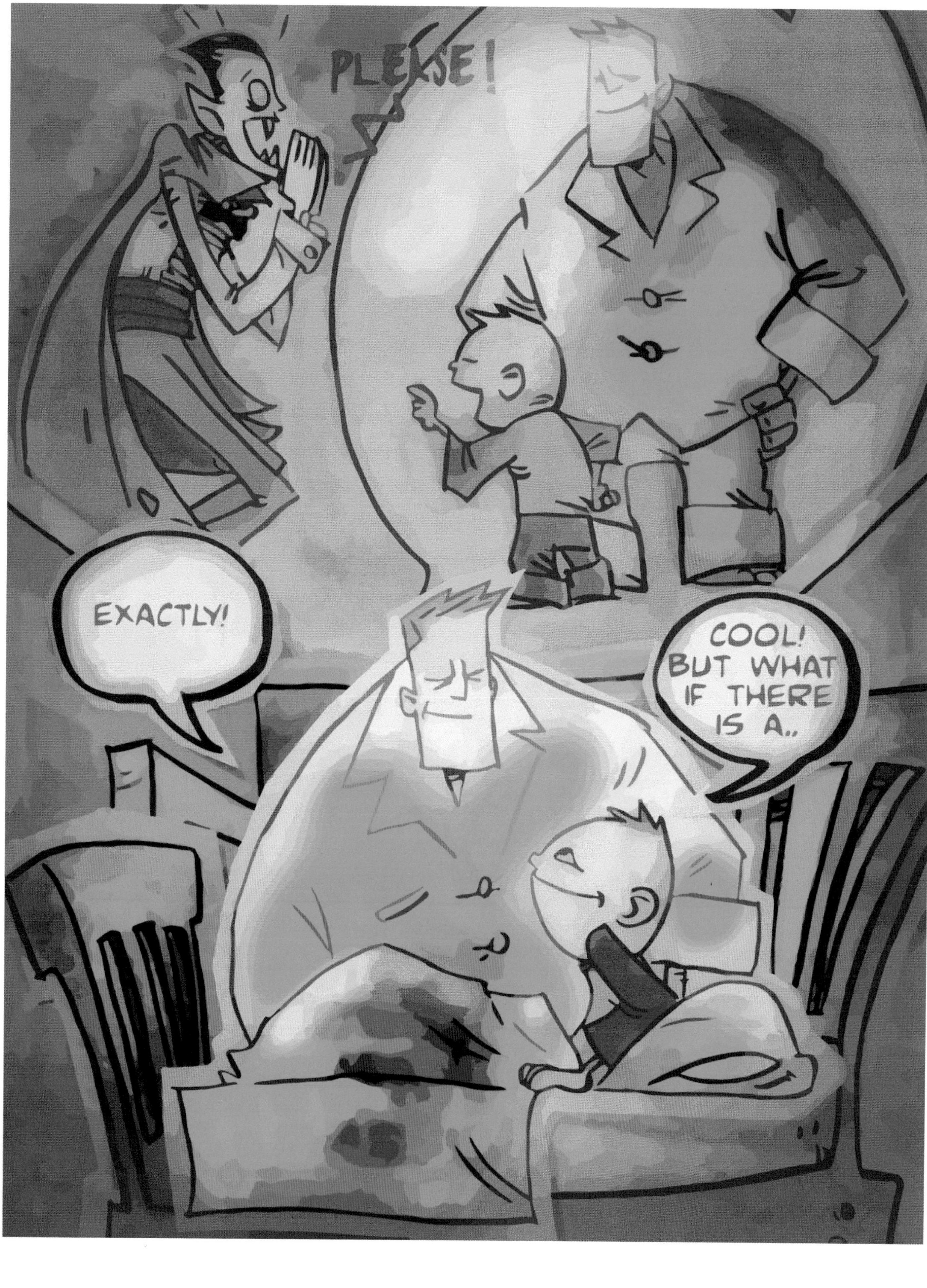
PLEASE!
EXACTLY!
COOL! BUT WHAT IF THERE IS A..

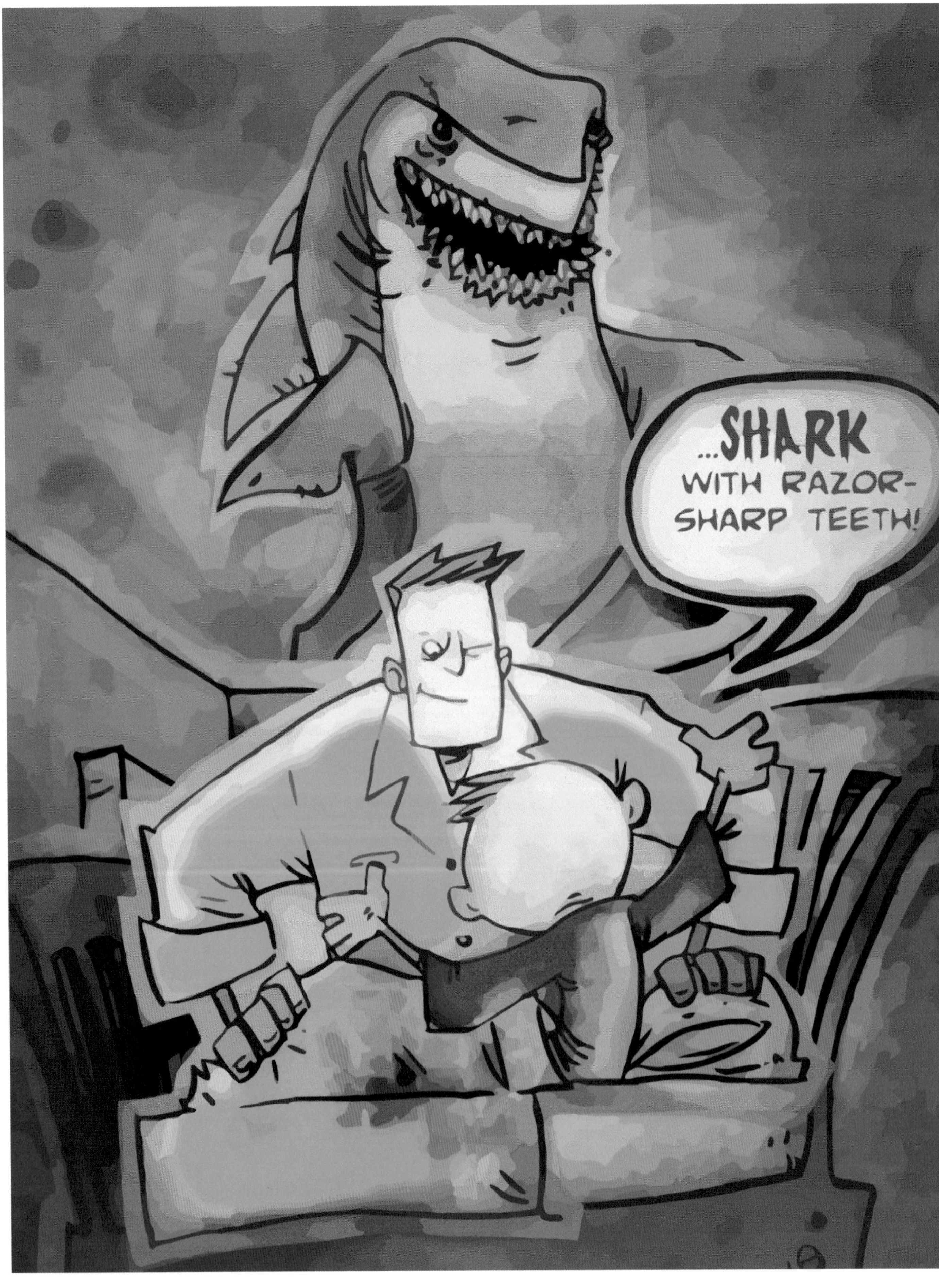
...SHARK WITH RAZOR-SHARP TEETH!

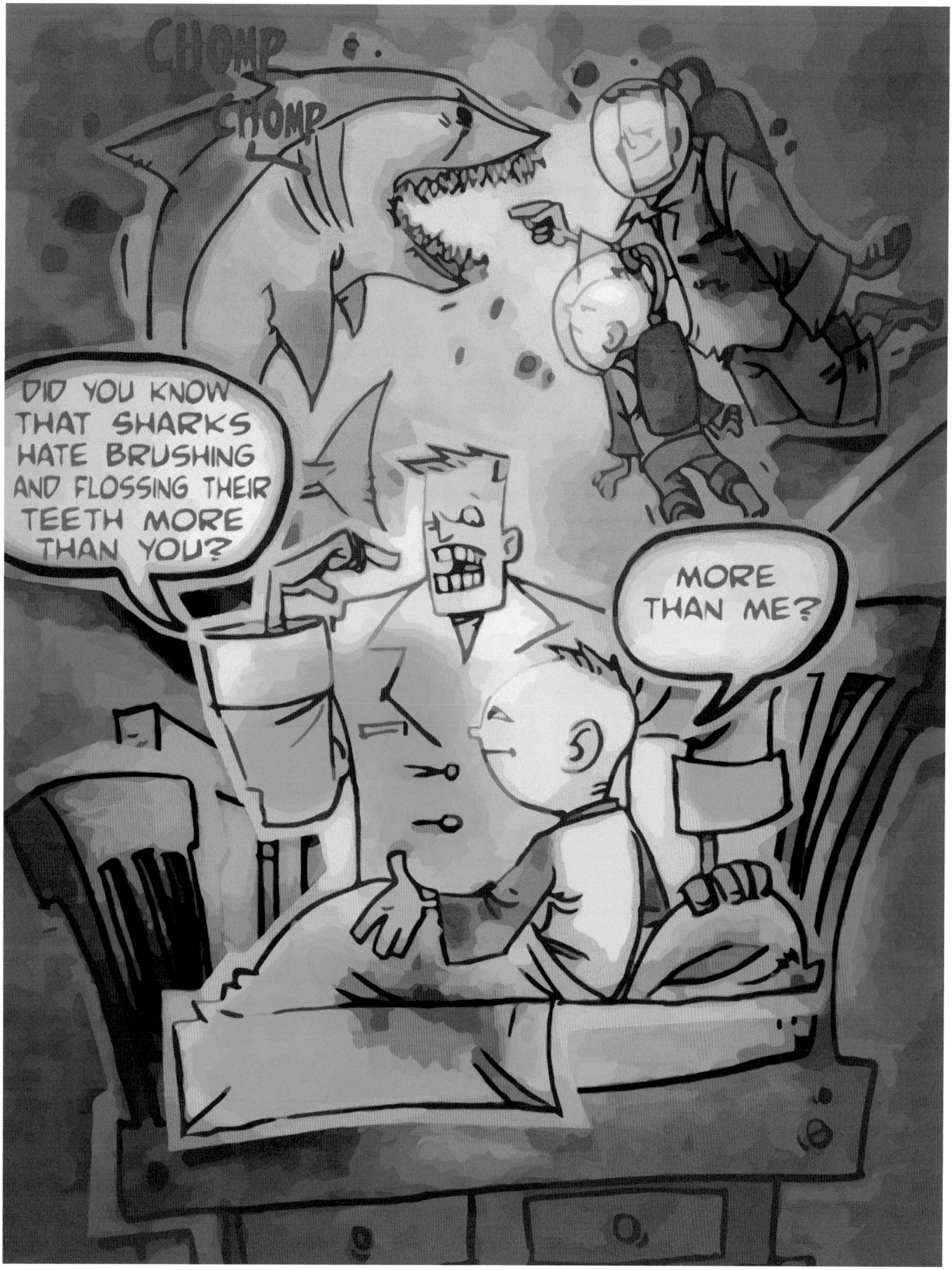
CHOMP
CHOMP
DID YOU KNOW THAT SHARKS HATE BRUSHING AND FLOSSING THEIR TEETH MORE THAN YOU?
MORE THAN ME?

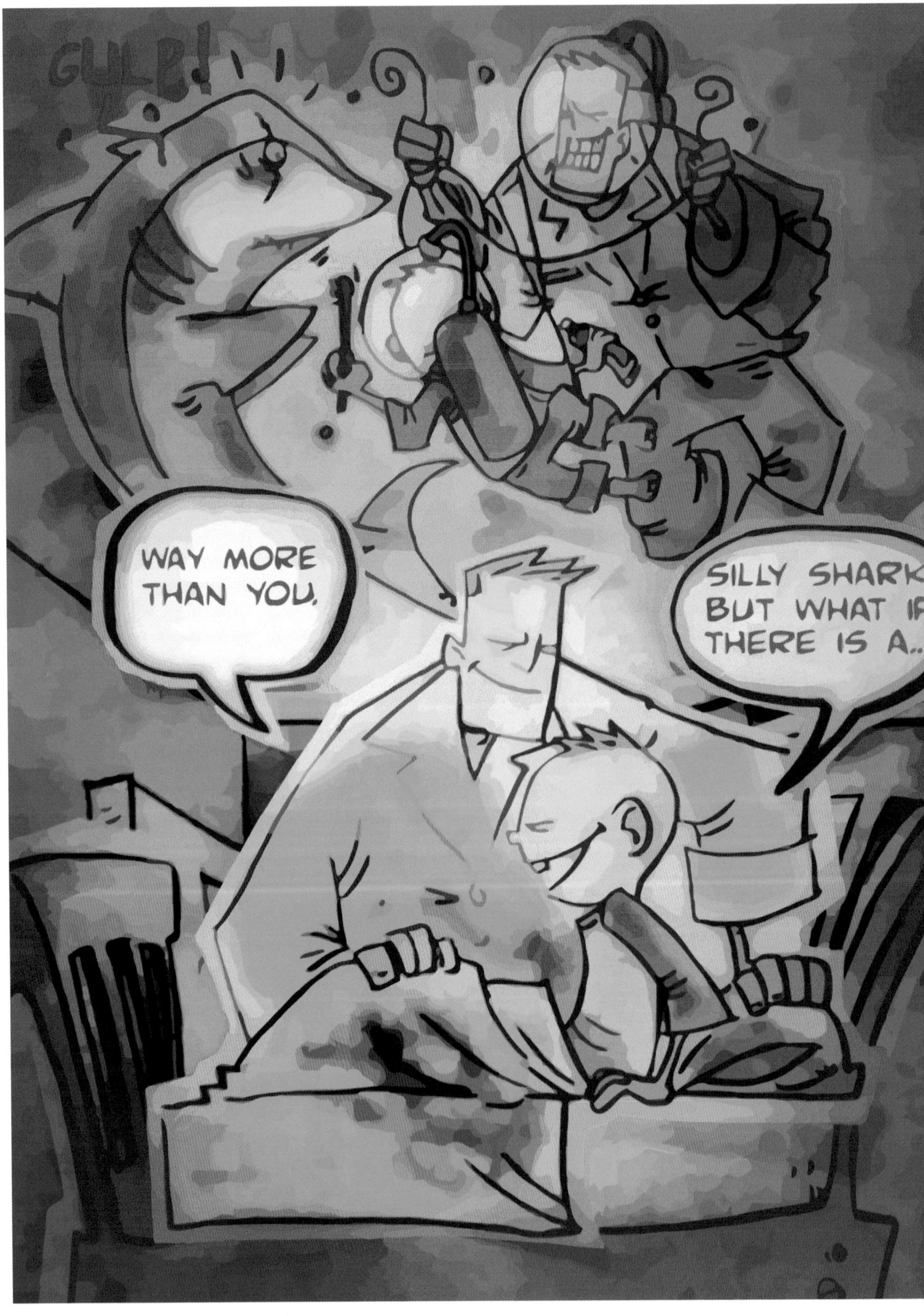
GULP!
WAY MORE THAN YOU.
SILLY SHARK. BUT WHAT IF THERE IS A...

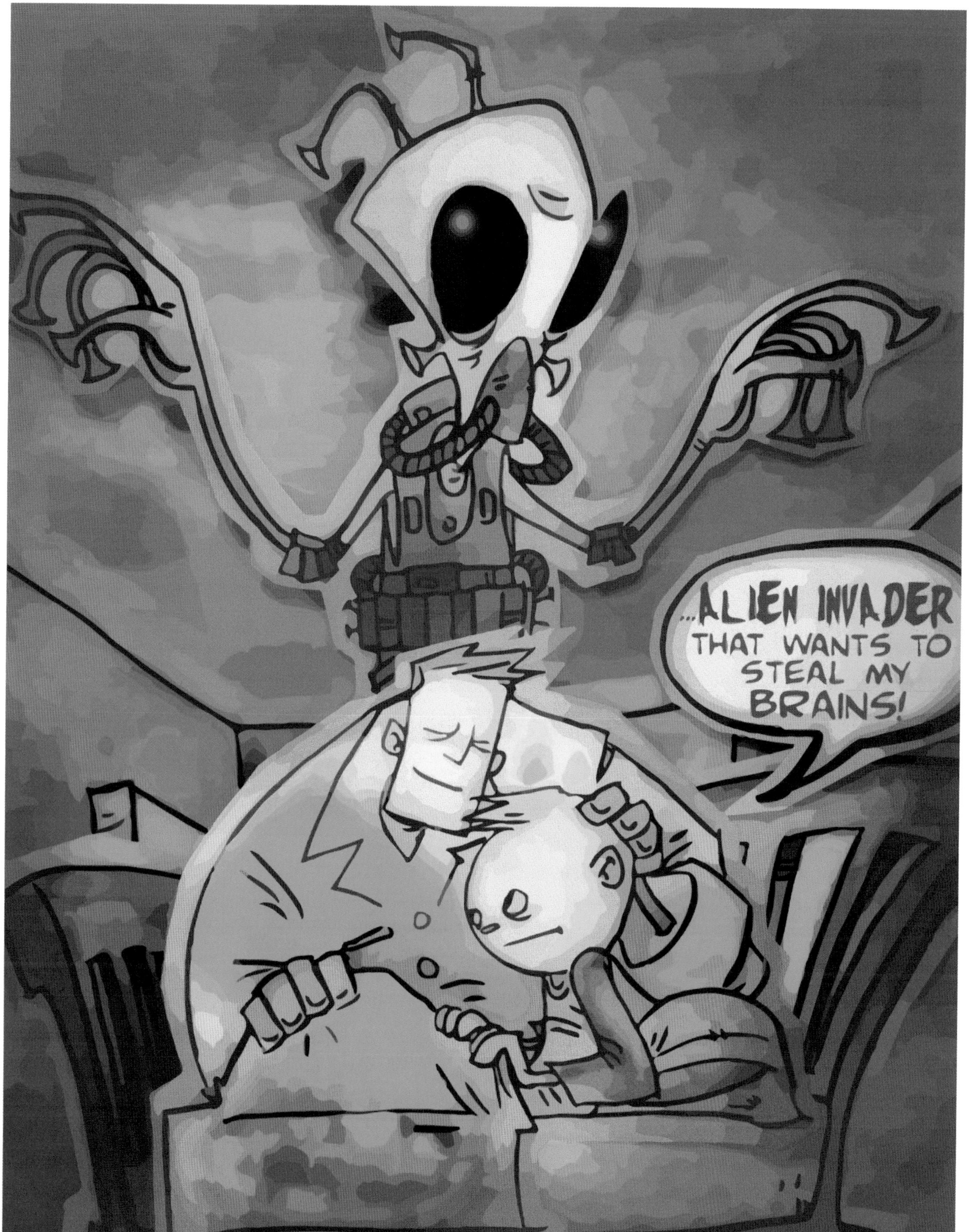
...ALIEN INVADER THAT WANTS TO STEAL MY BRAINS!

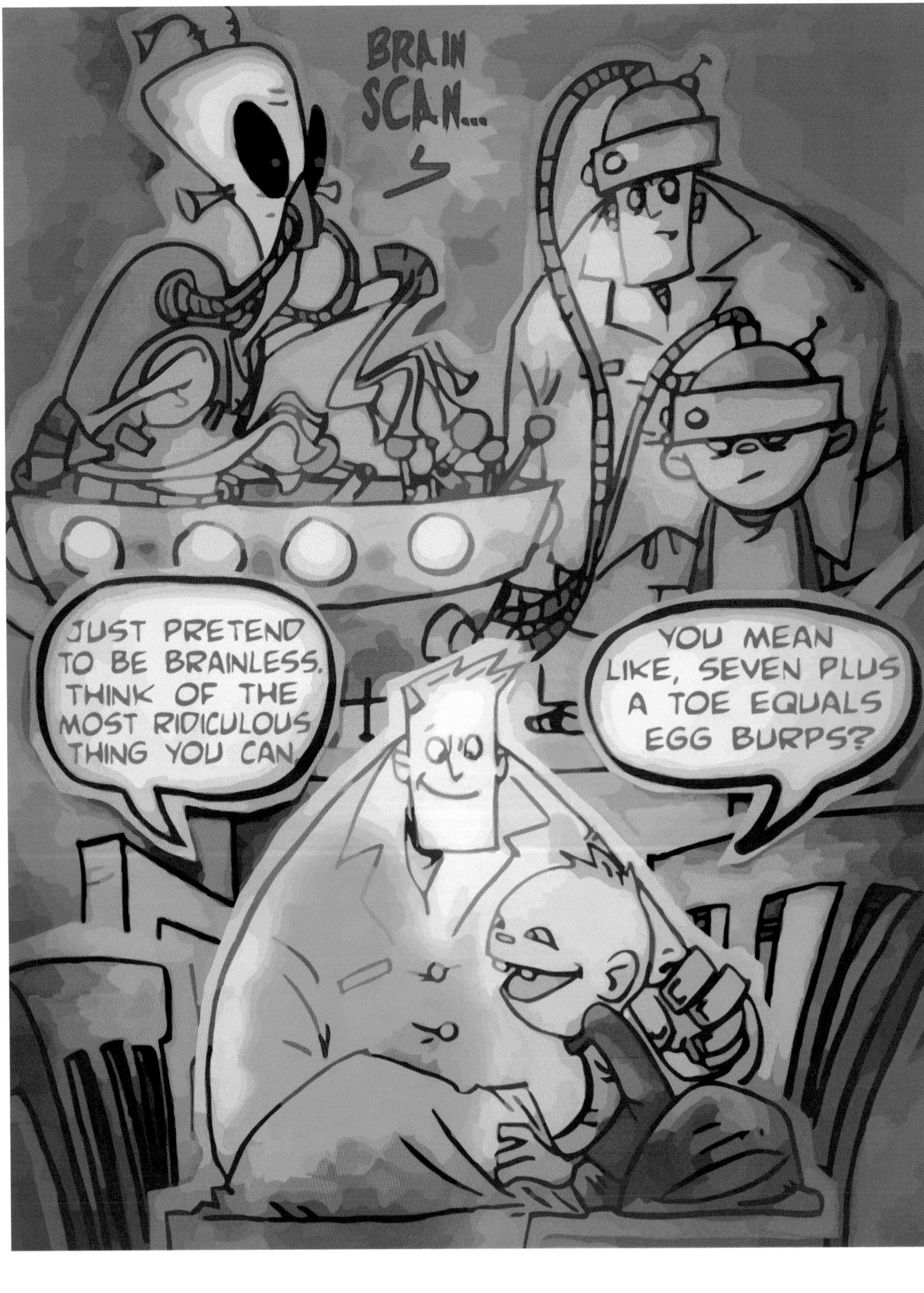
BRAIN SCAN...
JUST PRETEND TO BE BRAINLESS. THINK OF THE MOST RIDICULOUS THING YOU CAN.
YOU MEAN LIKE, SEVEN PLUS A TOE EQUALS EGG BURPS?

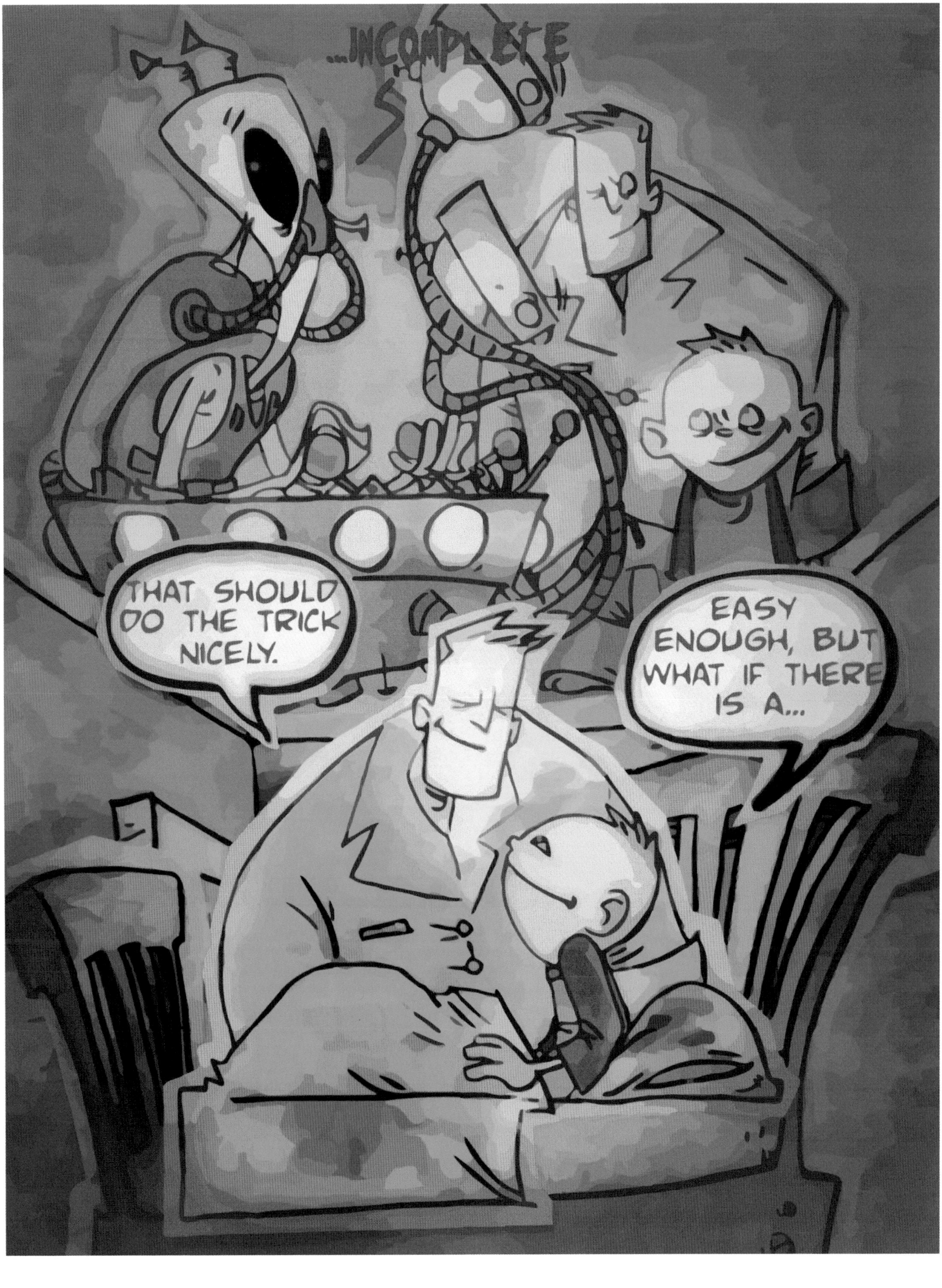
...INCOMPLETE
THAT SHOULD DO THE TRICK NICELY.
EASY ENOUGH, BUT WHAT IF THERE IS A...

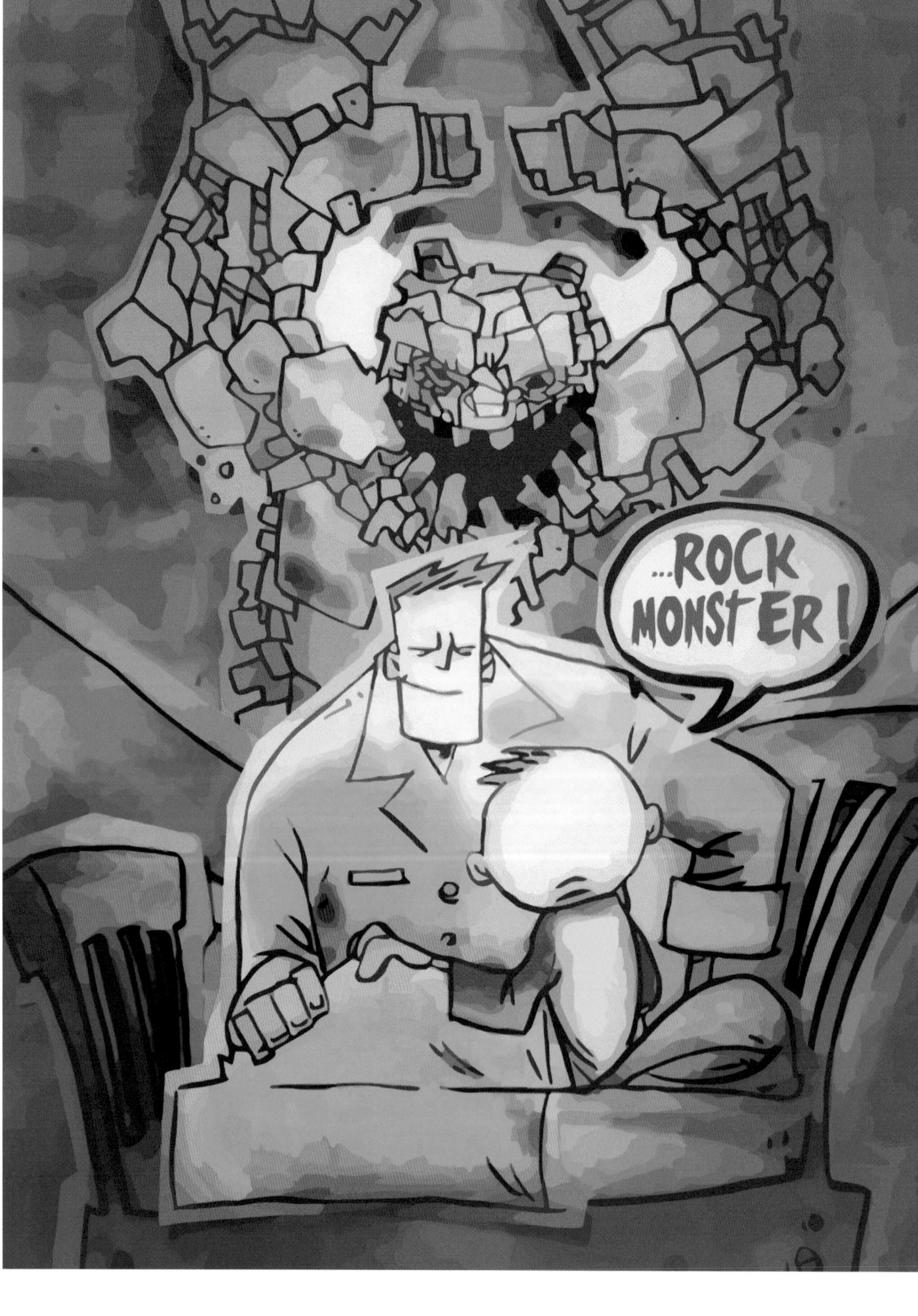
...ROCK MONSTER!

GRUMBLE
ROCK-PAPER-SCISSORS! ROCK-PAPER-SCISSORS! PAPER BEATS ROCK! PAPER AIRPLANES SHOULD DO THE TRICK!
PAPER AIRPLANES, REALLY?

OUCH!
REALLY! JUST THROW THAT AIRPLANE AND WATCH IT CRUMBLE!
CRUMBLE! CRUMBLE! BUT WHAT IF THERE IS A...

GOOEY GLOBSTER THAT WANTS TO SWALLOW ME UP WHOLE!

HEY, THAT'S MINE!
YUMMY! OKAY SON. LAST ONE. THEN IT'S TIME TO GO BACK TO SLEEP.

OKAY, THEN HOW ABOUT A SCARY GHOST DOG!

EASY. IT'S NOT POSSIBLE. IT'S A WELL KNOW-FACT ALL DOGS GO TO HEAVEN. ALRIGHT, TIME TO CLOSE YOUR EYES.
AWE MAN, THAT WAS TOO EASY!

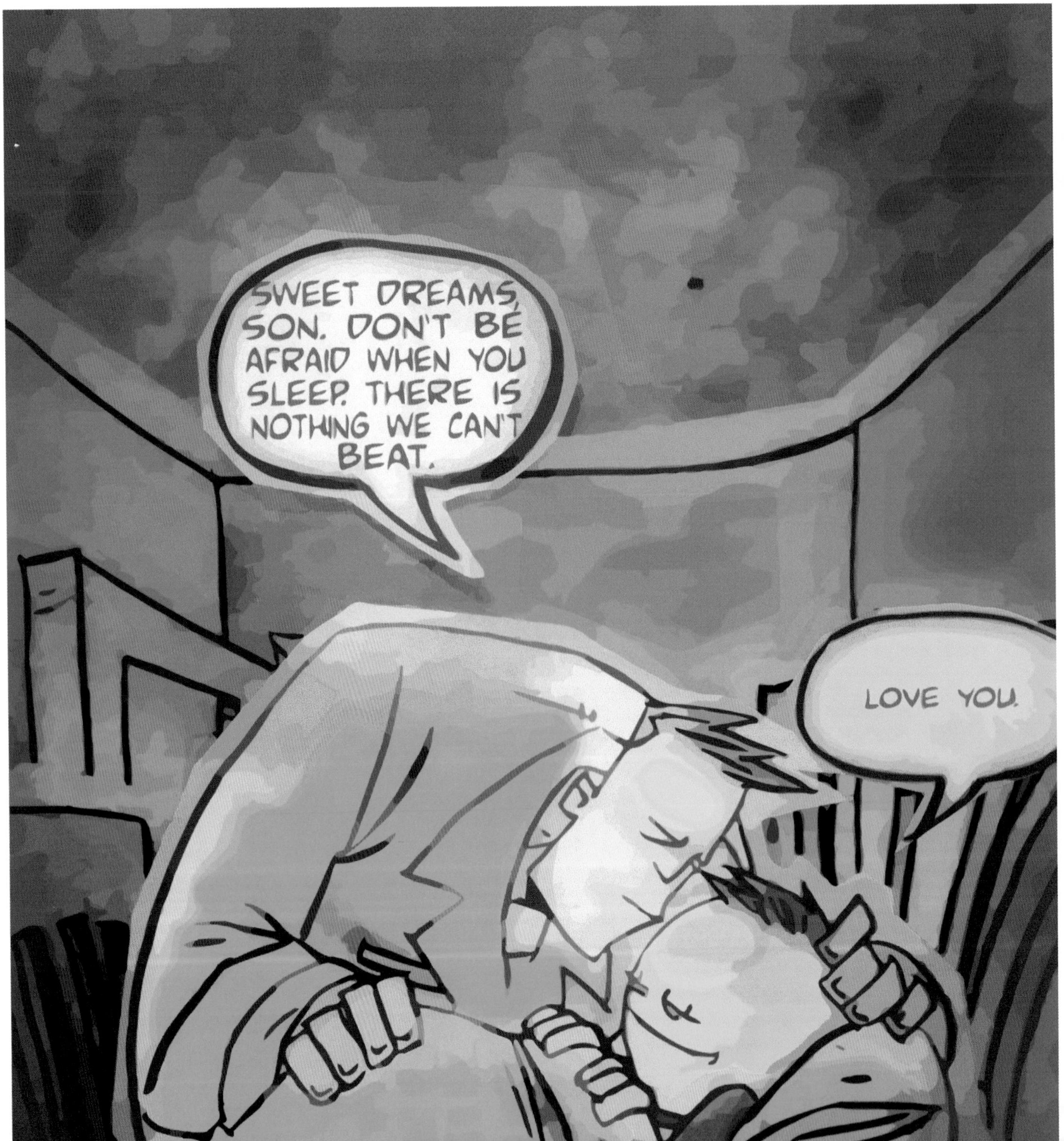
SWEET DREAMS, SON. DON'T BE AFRAID WHEN YOU SLEEP. THERE IS NOTHING WE CAN'T BEAT.
LOVE YOU.

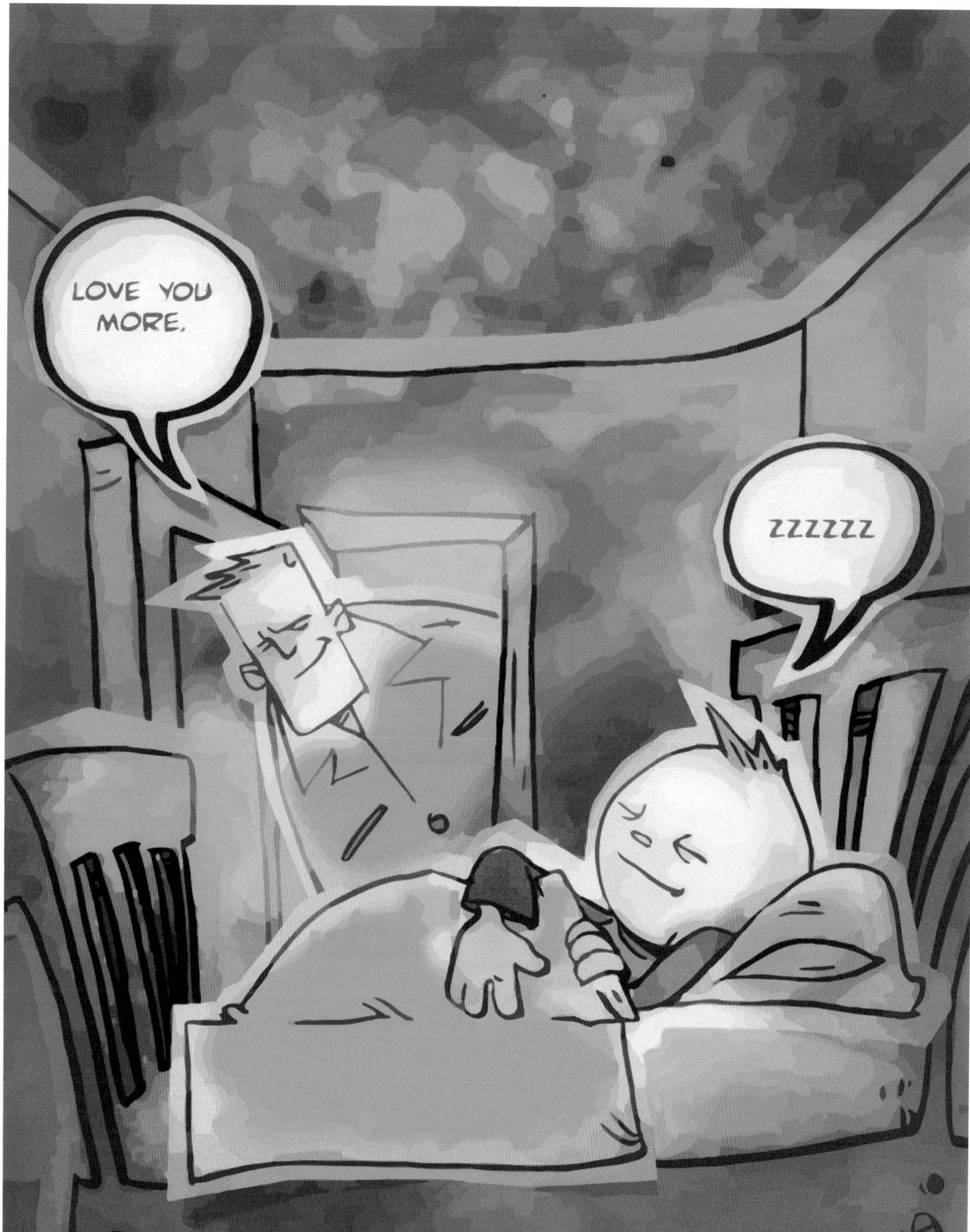
LOVE YOU MORE.
ZZZZZZ

39454801R00022

Made in the USA
Charleston, SC
05 March 2015